D1109598

Real Heroes Don't Wear Capes

by Laura Driscoll
illustrated by Amy Wummer

Kane Press, Inc.
New York

For all of my many teachers—L.D.

Acknowledgments: Our thanks to Sonia Levitin, educator and author of numerous books for children, young adults, and adults; creator of "Finding Our Heroes and Ourselves Through Literature: A Workshop for Teachers."

Library of Congress Cataloging-in-Publication Data

Driscoll, Laura.
  Real heroes don't wear capes / by Laura Driscoll ; illustrated by Amy Wummer.
      p. cm. — (Social studies connects)
  "History & culture/heroes-Grades: 1/3."
  "With fun activities!"
  Summary: Ethan sets out to bring fame and recognition to his pogo-stick hero, Boyd "Boing" Bower, but discovers that being a hero means more than being famous.
  ISBN-13: 978-1-57565-245-0 (alk. paper)
  ISBN-10: 1-57565-245-5 (alk. paper)
  [1. Pogo sticks—Fiction. 2. Heroes—Fiction.] I. Wummer, Amy, ill. II. Title.
  PZ7.D79Re 2007
  [Fic]—dc22
                                  2006102069

10 9 8 7 6 5 4 3 2 1

First published in the United States of America in 2007 by Kane Press, Inc.
Printed in Hong Kong.

Social Studies Connects is a registered trademark of Kane Press, Inc.

Book Design: Edward Miller

www.kanepress.com

Boing!! Boing!! Boing!!

"Forty-eight, forty-nine, fifty . . ." My friend Ben keeps count while I bounce on my pogo stick.

Fifty bounces! It's the most I've ever done!

My little brother, Dex, cheers me on. "Ethan! Go for sixty!"

But on fifty-six I lose my balance and hop off. "Fifty-six!" I yell. "It's my new record!"

I've been working on my bounce record for a whole week—ever since I got my new pogo stick. Bouncing makes me feel like I'm walking on the moon. I could bounce all day!

But Dex wants to try, so I help him climb on. Meanwhile, I fill Ben in on some pogo-stick trivia.

"Did you know that in the 1960s you could buy a pogo stick with a motor?" I tell Ben. "It could bounce twelve feet in the air!"

Ben laughs. "Ethan, how do you fit so many weird facts in your brain?"

Okay, so I'm a trivia nut. But you wouldn't believe the cool stuff most people don't know.

"Did you know that the longest piece of pasta ever made was 418 feet from end to end?" I ask the cafeteria lady. She's speechless.

"Did you know that scientists found a 160-million-year-old fossil of dinosaur vomit?" I tell Cindy Lopez on our field trip. I'm not sure she's listening, though, because she looks kind of pale—like she doesn't feel well.

"Did you know that Thomas Edison didn't like going to sleep, either?" I say to Dex, who is too wound up at bedtime. "Come on, I'll read to you about pogo sticks!"

I've taken out every book in the library on pogo sticks. I've already read *The Ups and Downs of Pogo Sticking* and *It's a Spring Thing*. Tonight I open *Pogomania!*—and that's when I see it.

FIRST
CROSS-COUNTRY
POGO-STICK TREK
*Incredible Journey
Across the U.S.*

Boyd "Boing" Bower
Plainville, CT
Record set on
June 22, 1922

"Hey, Dex!" I say. "This guy was from Plainville. From *our town!*" I flip the page.

"It says here that Boing Bower bounced
3,000 miles—through wind, rain, and snow, over
mountains and across deserts," I tell Dex. "It
took him six months to do it. What a hero!"

Dex's eyes get big. "Wow! Can we meet him?"

"I wish we could," I say. I explain about how
Boing lived a long life in Plainville, but that he
died in 1970.

Hero is a word you hear a lot.
What does it mean to you?

Dex finally falls asleep. I curl up in bed wondering why I've never heard of Boing Bower. I'll bet nobody else in Plainville has, either!

That night I dream that Boing and I are bouncing across the country. We bounce a hundred . . . a thousand . . . a million times! We keep bouncing until I lose count!

I wake up wanting to tell the whole world about Boing Bower. I start at the bus stop.

"What strength!" I say. "What balance! He's my pogo-stick hero!"

"Hero?" Kenny Spivey snorts. "Did he have a rocket-powered pogo stick and a cool cape?"

"Kenny," says Ben, "I think Ethan means a real-life hero, not a superhero."

Sure, it would be cool to fly or have x-ray vision. But superheroes and their powers are make-believe. Real-life heroes are real people who do special things.

Cindy Lopez pops her gum. "If he's a real hero," she says, "does he have a holiday named for him, like Dr. Martin Luther King Jr.?"

"Or a statue, like Abraham Lincoln's in the Lincoln Memorial?" asks Kenny.

"Or maybe there's stuff about him in a museum," says Ben, trying to be helpful. "Like Jackie Robinson in the Baseball Hall of Fame?"

I don't know what to say. I don't think Boing Bower has a holiday, a statue, or a spot in any museum. But he should!

In a little town like Plainville, we don't have many heroes. So I decide to write up a petition. Maybe if lots of kids sign it, Plainville will have a new holiday—Boing Bower Day!

Some holidays, like Martin Luther King Jr. Day, are named for American heroes. Dr. King worked hard to change laws that treated people unfairly because of the color of their skin. He helped make our country a better place for everyone.

At recess the next day, I hang up a poster and wait for kids to come over. But everyone seems more interested in kickball. How can I get their attention? Then it hits me. Trivia!

"Hey!" I call out. "Did you guys know that the longest attack of hiccups lasted 68 years?"

HONOR A
HOMETOWN
HERO!

Nobody seems to care . . . except one little kid. "I know that word," she says. "H-E-R-O. Hero. I have a hero!"

"Is it Boing Bower?" I ask.

"Huh?" she says. "No. It's Mrs. Lipton, my teacher. I was sick all last week, and she came to help me with my reading every day after school!"

I smile. "That's great. But do you want to sign my petition? I want to start a holiday for—"

The girl's eyes light up. "Great idea!" She takes my clipboard. "Hey, everybody!" she calls out. "Who thinks there should be a holiday called Mrs. Lipton Day?"

Lots of kids rush over. "We do!" they say.

Before I know it, my Boing Bower Day petition has become a Mrs. Lipton Day petition.

I decide to try something new. Did you know that most Americans eat more than fifty tons of food in their lives? That means supermarkets are busy places!

I set up a table outside Super Shop & Save. Maybe I can raise enough money for a Boing Bower statue.

BUILD A STATUE FOR A HOMETOWN HERO!

The biggest statue of an American hero is of Sam Houston in Huntsville, Texas. It's 67 feet tall! In the 1800s, Sam Houston was a soldier, congressman, senator, and governor. He worked for equal rights for Native Americans.

"Excuse me," I say to one lady. "Want to help honor a Plainville hero?"

She smiles. "All right. I'd like to honor my neighbor, Mr. Mott. He mows my lawn and cleans my gutters—and he won't take a penny for it!"

I explain about Boing Bower and the statue I want to build.

"Boing *who?*" she says.

The famous carvings on Mount Rushmore honor Presidents George Washington, Thomas Jefferson, Abraham Lincoln, and Theodore Roosevelt. It took 400 workers 14 years to finish the monument!

Everywhere I go, it's the same. No one wants
to know about *my* hero. But they all want to tell
me about *their* heroes.

At swim lessons, my instructor Padma asks
about the T-shirt I made. I tell her about Boing.
Then she tells me all about her cousin Vijay. "He
took me snorkeling in Blue Lake to help me get
over my fear of deep water," Padma says.

After Dex's soccer game, I pass out some BOING! buttons. I tell Dex's coach, Mr. Nealy, about Boing. Then he tells me about *his* hero— his dad, who worked three jobs so Mr. Nealy could go to college.

Ethan put his hero's name on buttons. Some American heroes are on stamps and coins—like Susan B. Anthony. She worked for many years to get women the right to vote.

My next idea is to make "Build It for Boing!" signs. I let Dex color in the letters.

But even at home I hear about other people's heroes. Mom looks at my signs and smiles.

"Ethan, you remind me of Mrs. Cho," she says. "You know, the lady who saved the old firehouse from being torn down? You're trying to save Plainville history, just like she did."

I know my mom is trying to be nice. But this isn't about Mrs. Cho! It isn't about Mrs. Lipton, Mr. Nealy's dad, Padma's swim teacher, or that supermarket lady's neighbor. I bet they are all great people. But this is about Boing Bower! I want everyone to know what a big hero he is!

I try to cheer up by looking for more Boing Bower trivia. I flip through *Far-Out Firsts* until I spot a photo of him. There's a caption, too.

Boyd "Boing" Bower (1898–1970) outside the Plainville school he helped build

In 1922 Boyd Bower pogo-sticked across the country and won the World's Wackiest Stunt contest. He gave all of his $5,000 prize money to help build the Plainville School. "I wasn't sure I'd make it," said Bower. "But folks back home needed the money, so that's what kept me bouncing."

What is a hero?
Ethan's hero is caring, helpful, and willing to work hard for other people. Do you know anyone like this?

"Unbelievable!" I say to myself. He was daring, determined, a great pogo-sticker . . . *and* he didn't even do it for himself. He bounced through the rain and snow and desert to help others!

Boing Bower was an even bigger hero than I'd thought!

But wait a minute. I think back to what everyone said about their own heroes.

First, they each worked hard to do something great for someone else—just like Boing Bower did.

Second . . . *none* of them are famous. There is no holiday for Mr. Nealy's dad. There is no statue of Padma's cousin. And I'll bet Mrs. Cho isn't in any museum. But maybe she could be. . . .

Maybe they *all* could be!

Not all famous people are heroes. And not all heroes are famous. Fame is about people knowing your name. Being a hero is about choosing to do the right thing—even when it's not easy or popular.

I forget the Boing statue. Now I want to build something else. I won't need any money. But I'll need help . . . from Mom . . .

from Mr. Nealy . . .

from Padma . . .

and from lots of other people, too.

It isn't long before the Plainville Hero Museum
is open for business . . . in our garage!

"What gave you the idea to do this?" the
Plainville News reporter asks me.

"Well," I reply, "it all started with a pogo-sticker
named Boing Bower. . . ."

Just as the reporter takes my picture, Dex tugs
at my shirt. "Ethan, can *my* hero be in the
museum?" he asks me.

"Sure!" I say. "Who is it?"

Dex smiles. "Guess!"

"Oh, okay," I say, scratching my head. But this
is one piece of trivia I don't know.

"It's you!" says Dex. "You let me bounce on your pogo stick even when *you* want to. You give me piggyback rides even when you're tired. You read to me at bedtime. You never miss my soccer games. And you do lots of other nice stuff for me."

Wow! Me? A hero? I don't know what to think. But I'm happy that Dex sees me that way.

I look around. Lots of other people look happy, too—happy to tell the town about their heroes.

Okay, so Plainville might never have a Boing Bower holiday or monument or museum.

But it *does* have a hero museum—and a whole lot of heroes.

You don't have to pogo across the country or change the world to be a hero. Anybody can be a hero—even you!

I can express ideas!

MAKING CONNECTIONS

Suppose you had an idea that you wanted to share. How would you express your idea? Would you talk it up? Write it down?

Ethan thinks that Boing deserves to be a town hero. He tries to convince people that his idea is a good one. He makes signs and T-shirts and buttons. How else could he have expressed his idea?

Look Back

- On page 14, what is Ethan's first idea? What does he do on page 15 to express his idea?
- How does Ethan try to get attention and express his ideas on pages 18–19?
- On page 27, Ethan gets a new idea. Look at pages 28–29. What was his new idea? Do you think it worked? Why?

Try This!

Be a hero! Pretend you want to pogo-stick across your neighborhood—or ride a unicycle, or hop on one foot, or whatever sounds like a fun challenge to you. How would you express your idea and convince people to get involved? Make flyers . . . put up posters . . . go door-to-door . . . ?

Bonus: Do it! Ask your parents, neighbors, and members of your community to sponsor your trek. Then use the money you raise for a good cause—like a hero museum!